FROM A KA-BAR
TO THE CROSS

FROM A KA-BAR TO THE CROSS

CARSON BRANNAN

ReadersMagnet, LLC

From a KA-BAR to the Cross.
Copyright © 2022 by Carson Brannan

Published in the United States of America
ISBN   Paperback: 978-1-956780-41-3
ISBN   eBook: 978-1-956780-40-6

All rights reserved. No part of this publication may be reproduced, stored in a retrieval system or transmitted in any way by any means, electronic, mechanical, photocopy, recording or otherwise without the prior permission of the author except as provided by USA copyright law.

The opinions expressed by the author are not necessarily those of ReadersMagnet, LLC.

ReadersMagnet, LLC
10620 Treena Street, Suite 230 | San Diego, California, 92131 USA
1.619. 354. 2643 | www.readersmagnet.com

Book design copyright © 2022 by ReadersMagnet, LLC. All rights reserved.
Cover design by Kent Gabutin
Interior design by Renalie Malinao

DEDICATION

This book is dedicated to the memory of my good friend Dan Goodman. He served his country honorably in the Vietnam conflict.

Part of my story is based on his experience at a forward fire base in Vietnam. Dan lived up to his name sake he was indeed a good man. He was always ready to lend a hand to those in need or to tell a joke if the conversation started to get stale. He died as a result of exposure to Agent Orange. A defoliant used in Vietnam.

Dan leaves behind a wife, a son, a daughter, and two grandchildren. He will be missed and never forgotten by anyone who knew him.

The United States of America
honors the memory of
Daniel J. Goodman
This certificate is awarded by a grateful nation in recognition of devoted and selfless consecration to the service of our country in the Armed Forces of the United States.

President of the United States

CONTENTS

Dedication v
Introduction xi

A Preachers Story 1
Vietnam 7
The Long, Long Night 9
By The Dawn's Early Light 11
Careful What You Wish For 14
Welcome to the Jungle 19
Friend or Foe 21
Daylight Disaster 23
Safe or Sorry 25
Hell in the Afternoon 29
Amazing Grace 31
From Hell to Halleluiah 33
The Rebirth of Ken Wilson 36
America the Beautiful 39
Laser Focus 41

Postscript 43

INTRODUCTION

A KA-Bar is a tool, or more specifically a knife. It is nine inches long with a six-inch blade; it has many functions: It is used to cut wood for fires and shelter. It is used to cut cloth for bandages and slings. It is used to cut the rope to tie things together. It is even used to open a soldier's k-rations, but its primary function is to cut and rip flesh. It is a soldier's last line of defense against an enemy adversary that wants to do him harm.

Sergeant Kenneth Wilson or Sarge to his friends didn't just like his KA-Bar, he loved it. He had used it effectively on many occasions in combat and it had never let him down. So, what would make him give up his survival knife for an old wooden cross? There are lessons to be learned between these pages, lessons of love, lessons of forgiveness, lessons about survival, both physical and emotional. Ken's journey *from a KA-Bar to the Cross* is not for the faint of heart, but it is an exciting trip.

A PREACHERS STORY

My name is Reverend Kenneth Paul Wilson, formerly known as Sergeant Kenneth Wilson or Sarge for short, of the elite U.S. Army Green Berets. I'm the preacher at a picturesque little white Church in the foothills of East Tennessee. How I became a preacher only God knows, but that's what this story is about. First, let me tell you a little about myself. I am six foot two with blonde hair and blue eyes, and even though I have been out of the service for years I still run two miles a day and work out at least three times a week.

For the most part, my sermons are very traditional, but every Memorial Day I take the congregation on a journey through a part of my life. It's a journey. From *a KA-Bar to the Cross*. I dedicate these sermons to those brave men and women who either didn't return from Vietnam or returned in a flag-draped coffin.

It's been said that my Memorial Day sermons are full of passion, with the conviction only a person who has walked through "the Valley of the Shadow of Death", and has come out on the other side, could use. All I know is that I preach from my heart. These sermons are sometimes long but certainly not boring. They are more stories than sermons per se, but they are filled with love. They are stories of the love of a man for his fellow man and the love of a man for his God.

I shall start the story of my journey. From *a Ka-Bar to the Cross* much farther back than I ever do in my sermons. I will start back in my childhood, so you will get a better understanding of just how big a miracle it is that I am a preacher today.

My parents had not been church-going people, and I had grown up in a pretty rough neighborhood in south-central L.A. I lost my two best friends to gang violence before I was twelve. Jimmy O'Brien was a tough little kid. He was short for eleven, but he was wiry and quick. He had red hair and freckles, and he stood about 4 feet tall.

Jimmy's parents were first-generation Irish immigrants and he spoke with a serious Irish brogue. He was a good student, and his goal in life was to own his own grocery store.

Shawn Baker on the other hand was five foot eight, with brown hair and blazing blue eyes. He wore a size 10 shoe; and was a bit gangly, as though he hadn't quite grown into his body yet. He was fun-loving and full of life. Everyone enjoyed having him around because he was always helpful, kind, and he was a born storyteller. He dreamed of becoming an author when he grew up. I was kind of in-between and we looked like stair steps walking down the street. I had no idea what I wanted to do with my life. The only thing I knew was that as soon as I was old enough, I was going to move out of the hood.

On the afternoon of March 15th, 1958, the three of us were walking home from school, as we did every day. We had roughly a mile and three-quarters to walk. The school bus didn't start picking up children unless they lived two miles from school or farther.

As we rounded the corner of a street about a half-mile from home the street looked different than we had ever seen it before.

Normally there would be people sitting on the stoops of their row houses and kids playing kickball in the street, but not on that day. The street was abandoned. The sidewalks in this neighborhood were usually congested with people talking, smaller children playing around their mother's feet, bikes lying about as though abandoned by their owners, and an assortment of other stuff. To avoid the congestion on the sidewalk the three of us would walk down the middle of the street.

We were about halfway down the block when Jimmy said what we were all thinking, "This is really weird. It's like a scene from The Twilight Zone."

He no sooner got the words out of his mouth than I saw what appeared to be a bumblebee fly right by my nose. I could feel the rush of air it caused on my eyelashes. The sight was followed almost instantaneously by the unmistakable sound of a gunshot.

"Jimmy, Shawn, run! Run!!"

I didn't realize I was shouting until the sound of my voice came reverberating off the nearby buildings. From that point forward my life would never be the same.

Shawn being the tallest one in the group made the easiest target. He never got a chance to take a step before I saw the side of his head explode, and he fell where he stood. Jimmy and I ran for all we were worth, bullets whizzing by our heads. We were almost to the corner of the street when I heard Jimmy cry out. I turned my head just in time to see him fall face-first to the pavement. I thought about stopping to check on him, but I saw guys with guns pouring into the street from behind parked cars. They were still shooting in my direction, so I rounded the corner and didn't stop running until I got home.

The nightly news said the killings were gang violence, but Jimmy, Shawn, and I weren't part of any gangs. What's worse, no one was ever charged with the crimes. I grew up bitter, believing that the law of the jungle was the most important. Having not grown up in the church I believed when you died that was it, which made the loss of my friends that much harder to take.

My junior high and high school days were filled with fighting and rebellion against a world that I felt was unjust. My folks divorced when I was sixteen and I spent my last couple of years of school with my mom. Mom worked as a waitress at a local diner, but the money she made was never enough to get us through the month. So, I would work at whatever jobs were available. I flipped burgers at the local diner, I worked at a salvage yard, and I even spent some time on a fishing boat where I learned the value and usefulness of a good knife. When the money ran out, I would beg, borrow, or steal whatever we needed to get us through.

My mother said that I underwent a metamorphosis seemingly overnight, from a sweet innocent child to a bitter spiteful teenager. By the time I graduated high school I was well acquainted with the local gendarme.

I graduated from high school, but just barely. Three weeks after graduation I got a letter in the mail saying Uncle Sam wants you to join the Army. Mom had a sister in Cleveland, Ohio that was widowed and had a big house. She had asked Mom to come and live with her, but Mom had hesitated to take the invitation because of me. My life wasn't going anywhere in L.A., and I knew Mom would be better off in Ohio, so I went down to the local recruiting office and joined up. Mom wasn't pleased with my decision, because there was a war going on, but she accepted it and made plans to go live with her sister when I left.

The Army cut orders for me to report to Fort Benning, GA. to begin my basic training. Uncle Sam was even nice enough to buy me a one-way non-refundable ticket on a Greyhound bus from L.A. to G.A. The trip took two full days. I had never been out of L.A. and some of the sceneries were amazing. When I fell asleep the first night I awoke to a whole new vista outside my window. I wondered what else I might see during my Army days. Some of the things I saw while I was in the Army were awe-inspiring for their beauty, and some things were unforgettable for their horror.

I wasn't used to taking orders from anyone, and I would rather fight than listen. So, the first week or two of boot camp were, let's just say, not pleasant. Once I accepted my fate I found the structure and discipline a refreshing change from what I had known Growing up in L.A. I think the hardest lesson for me to learn, was to trust others. In Los Angeles, I learned not to trust anyone, so the concept of trusting your fellow soldier with your life was very foreign indeed. My street fighting in L.A. helped me when we went through our hand-to-hand combat training, and I excelled in the use of a KA-Bar which I found to be a very well-made knife. After boot camp, I was assigned to a base specializing in big guns, howitzers, and the like. As my training progressed, I found the instruction manuals were put together in a matter-of-fact way that was easy to understand. I was able to climb the ranks fairly easily and made the rank of Sergeant in almost record time.

One day I saw a notice on the barracks bulletin board announcing that applications were being accepted for the Green Berets training school. I immediately put in a request to my company commander asking if I could apply. Once he received my request, he sent word for me to report to his office.

"Sergeant Wilson reporting as ordered Sir."

"Come in son. Take a seat. I see you want to join the Green Berets. Why is that?" "Sir, I believe that I could do a good job as a Green Beret. I did well in my survival training and I was at the top of my class in hand-to-hand combat."

"I agree with you Son. There's only one thing I'm concerned about and that's your anger. You have some issues. You've been written up twice for bar fights and you were implicated in at least three others. Son, you almost lost your sergeant strips before you earned them. All that being said; if you could focus that intensity in a positive and controlled manner, I think you'd make a hell of a Green Beret."

"Sir, I know I have an anger problem and I believe that the military has helped me to control it. The discipline and structure have been good for me. Sir, I haven't been in a fight or even an argument for three or four months. Whenever I start to get angry, I simply take out my K-Bar and start sharpening it. For some reason that calms me right down. I believe my life experience will help me become all that I can be as a Green Beret."

"Be all that you can be. That sounds like it would make a good recruiting slogan.

Okay, Son, I'm going to grant your request and I will send my recommendation along with your transfer. Don't let me down, Sergeant Wilson."

"I won't Sir. Thank you, thank you very much."

I was accepted and shipped out within a week.

While at Special Forces training in Fort Bragg North Carolina, I met Jack Sullivan.

He was quiet, but he proved to be a very able soldier. I didn't make friends easily, but there was something about Jack that I liked. By the end of our training, Jack and I were best of friends and when the time came to get our assignments, we were able to convince the C.O. to have us assigned to the same unit. All Green Berets rotated into Vietnam. We were the best the Army had to offer, and it just made sense to use us where we could do the most good.

VIETNAM

Now let me fast forward to 1969 near the city of Da Nang, South Vietnam.
I was part of an exploratory unit with the U.S. Army Green Berets. Our job was to locate "Charlie", military jargon for the Viet Cong guerilla fighters, also known as V.C., without being detected. After locating the enemy, we would call in artillery or airstrikes on the enemy position. This worked most of the time, but on more occasions, than I care to remember, the enemy forces would discover my men and me. The enemy units we were trying to locate would generally outnumber our small band of men by sometimes as little as two to one or as much as a hundred to one. Once we were discovered, the clandestine assignment would turn into a life-or-death firefight.

This wasn't my first rodeo, as the saying goes. It was my fifth tour of duty in Vietnam. I had lost a lot of good men and a few close friends during my time in country. I had learned how to overcome incredible fear, and I also learned how to put on a shell of non-feeling, as most combat veterans do, to survive the physical and moreover the emotional rigors of war. No matter how chaotic or even gory a combat situation became, I was all business all the time. This persona made me seem invincible to the new men in my squad. What they didn't know was that I was just as scared as they were; I had just learned how to hide it better. Normally the Army would rotate a soldier out of Vietnam after one or two tours, but Jack and I were good at what we did, and we volunteered to come back whenever we could. The Army regulations were bent if not broken to let us come back so many times.

I was, to put it politely, a hell-raiser. I used my R&R as an escape valve from the horrors and the pressures of combat. I drank too much, gambled too much, and I knew more than my share of Bargirls from Saigon to Singapore.

If you have never experienced war firsthand, please don't judge me too harshly. War is as close to Hell as any man will experience on this earth. Some never escape the hell of war even years after they have left the battlefields.

I'm not looking for forgiveness when I tell my story. I am relating it to you not that you might judge, but that you might learn. Learn how a man that knew sin and all its trappings; A man that had taken not just one life with his hands, like Cain, but many lives, without remorse, or even a flicker of conscience. How a man like that could find the Lord in the middle of a battlefield.

THE LONG, LONG NIGHT

Now, where was I? Oh yes, I remember. It was 5 June 1969. The weather was like it always is during June in South Vietnam, hot and humid. Imagine trying to work inside a pressure cooker. That's what it was like to be a foot soldier in Vietnam. I, my good friend Lance Corporal Jack Sullivan, who I had served with since 1966, and six newly assigned Green Berets fresh out of training and only in-country for a few days, where to go on a recon mission at first light.

I wasn't comfortable with greenhorns on my patrols, but Jack and I were good teachers, so we generally got stuck with at least a few in our squad. Once we taught them the things, they don't teach you in boot camp or even Green Beret training, our Commanding Officer would rotate them out and give us a new batch to train. We didn't like this, but we had learned to live with it. The C.O. had tried to transfer Jack once, but I made such a stink that he reconsidered.

Our base camp was 10 miles due west of the airbase at Da Nang. Da Nang Air-force Base was a juicy target, and "Charlie" was always trying to penetrate the defenses around the base. That's why my men and I were there. It was our job to stop the V.C. before they could get too close to the base.

The night before a mission was always long and most of the men got very little sleep. Some of the men would write to their loved ones. Some of them would spend a good deal of time in prayer; this was where Jack Sullivan could usually be found. Some of the men would stay up half the night playing cards to try and get their minds off of the mission to come.

The life expectancy for a green soldier in Vietnam was not very good. There were pun-gee sticks, tripwires, antipersonnel mines, and snipers. Not to mention a plethora of poisonous snakes and insects. This fact did not escape the new men in our unit. The fact that they'd been trained as Green Berets gave them a distinct advantage over the typical soldier fresh out of basic training, but it by no means, ensured their survival. I did what I always did before a mission. I broke down and cleaned every part of my M-16 machine gun and my .45 handgun. After putting them back together and assuring that they were in good working order, I'd put together the items I thought we'd need for the mission, and then I'd sharpen my Ka-Bar. I'd stay up sharpening my knife until the wee hours of the morning. I knew there were two things I could depend on. One was Jack, and the other was my trusty Ka-Bar. Neither one had ever let me down, and the three of us had been in some pretty tight spots.

BY THE DAWN'S EARLY LIGHT

O5:00 6 June 1969 Jack, I, and the rest of the men headed out on patrol. Our job was never safe, or easy, but on this day, it could be tougher than usual. An enemy radio transmission had been intercepted that suggested a company size unit of the North Vietnamese Army, more commonly referred to as NVA, were working their way down the valley that me and my men were assigned to check out. The valley in question was a little north and west of the base that we were assigned to, and although we couldn't be certain, it stood to reason, that Da Nang Air Base was the logical target for this force of NVA.

Just before we headed out Jack took me aside and said, "We have' t dealt with an enemy force this size since the Tet Offensive."

"Your right old friend. I hadn't thought of it until now, but you're exactly right." A couple of the guy's overheard Jack mention the Tet Offensive and persuaded him to tell the story.

"Ok here goes. During the Tet Offensive, the Sarge and I were assigned to a forward artillery base just south of the DMZ.

(DMZ is short for the demilitarized zone which was a no-man's zone between North and South Vietnam.) The Tet Offensive was a coordinated attack on allied forces all over South Vietnam. The base that the Sarge and I were at was besieged for a week straight. The base ran short on food, but more importantly, it ran short on ammunition. They called for resupply and reinforcements, but because the offensive was going on simultaneously all over the country, it was hard for Command and Control to coordinate supplies and reinforcements in a timely fashion.

On the sixth day, our base ran out of ammo for the big guns and mortars. Almost simultaneously, the men ran out of bullets for their personal weapons, and the fuel for the generators that powered the lights which illuminated the camp and surrounding terrain ran dry.

The base was surrounded by a ten-foot-tall, barbed wire fence with sandbags piled four feet high at the base. This was our first line of defense. About ten yards inside the perimeter of the base were a series of trenches that would act as a fallback position for the troops. On the last day before the attack that would inevitably come, the men used post-hole diggers to dig four-foot-deep vertical holes every six feet or so along the bottom of the trenches. The ground was then shaped so a grenade tossed into the trench would, hopefully, roll down into one of the holes before exploding. This would cause most of the power of the explosion and the shrapnel to go straight up sparing the men in the trench.

It was a beautiful sunset as I recall, but I knew that as soon as it was dark, the NVA that had been pounding us for the past week would be making their charge. As night fell the tension mounted. On the whole base, there were only twenty hand grenades, and a hand full of forty-fives that some of the soldiers carried. In total, there were just a couple dozen rounds of ammo for each pistol.

The base was manned by about equal numbers of Marines and Soldiers totaling approximately sixty officers and enlisted men.

I could hear my heart beating in my chest. I had butterflies in my stomach, and the palms of my hands started to sweat. If any man on the base said he wasn't afraid, he would have been lying just to make himself feel better. On that beautiful starlit night, thoughts of the home ran through my head, and I wished I was back in the States.

It was a new moon, and you could cut the darkness with a knife. Sergeant Wilson is very good with a KA-Bar, and he could cut almost anything with it, but even he couldn't cut the darkness of that night. The night birds were quiet, and a deafening stillness fell over the camp. I strained to see through the darkness. I listened intently, for the sounds of movement on the sides of the hill, on top of which the Base was situated. We all knew it was just a matter of time before the NVA would make their charge up the hill toward the base. Waiting was always the hardest part of a battle for me. I prayed, but the Sarge just sat on an empty ammo can and mumbled something about wanting to get to it and let the chips fall where they may.

CAREFUL WHAT YOU WISH FOR

Suddenly the night was split by the light of a half dozen flares. The enemy had fired the flares to light up the base. The NVA knew that the base had not been re-supplied for more than a week and they were feeling very confident that the base was out of ammo. As the North Vietnamese stormed up the hill toward the base the men with the forty-fives held fire and when the sea of men got close enough the grenades started flying. This provided only a momentary delay of the charge as the exploding grenade ripped big holes in the sea of soldiers charging up the hill. The front line of NVA reached the barbed wire surrounding the base about the same time the flares burned out. Sarge and I both figured, there were at least two hundred men staging the charge, and now the time had run out. The enemy was at the fence and there was no way to stop them except with the forty-fives, fire axes, mattocks, shovels, and the KA-Bars each man was issued in boot camp.

Most soldiers, me included, thought they would never have to use their KA-Bar, so they paid little attention during the phase of training that covered hand-to-hand combat, and did only as much as was required to pass that phase of their training. Sarge, on the other hand, paid very close attention and was almost picked as an instructor right out of boot camp.

Time was up, and as the NVA charged into the camp, guns blazing. Sarge and I hunkered down in one of the trenches and waited for our chance to strike.

"Here Jack, take my .45 and I'll use my KA-Bar.' "Are you sure Sarge?"

"Yes, Jack. If memory serves, I seem to remember you cutting yourself with your KA-Bar during training."

"Ok, your right. I am much better with a .45 than I am with a knife."

The smell of gun powder permeated the air and the cries of wounded and dying men along with the sound of weapons firing filled the night. The only light was from the muzzles of the guns firing. The scene was one of chaos and death. It reminded me of scenes from Dante's Inferno.

The contour of the ground in front of the trench that the Sarge and I were in, formed of a slight rise just before the trench. This along with the fact that it was as dark as a tomb made it almost impossible for the enemy to see the trench until they were right on top of it. This fact played right into our hands. The moment an enemy soldier stepped over the rise they were committed. They either had to jump over the trench or fall into it. The enemy reached our position two by two, and two by two the Sarge and I terminated them. Every time we killed two more, we would take their AK-47s and pass them to some of the other GI's that were in the trench with us so they could use the guns to repel the invaders.

"Pass the word along to the other men to take the AK-47s from the enemy and use their weapons against them," Sarge, shouted over the sound of the gunfire.

It's one thing to drop a man at two hundred yards and quite another to be nose to nose when you kill him. The fighting in the trenches was up close and personal.

There were no do-overs or free passes. Once an enemy soldier was in the trench it was either you or him. You either got it right or you were dead. The smell of human blood had mixed with the smell of gunpowder, mud, and human excrement, to form a pungent, almost nauseating odor in the trench that the Sarge and I were in. The dead and dying NVA in the trench made it hard for us to maneuver. Somehow, we managed and kept on fighting.

By the time the melee was over and the NVA had been repulsed, the body count was one hundred sixteen NVA dead and fourteen captured. The American casualties were twelve Marines, and ten Army Soldiers dead. Thirty U.S. Troops were wounded to one extent or another. Twelve of the NVA died as a direct result of Sarge and his KA-Bar. The enemy left the base alone for the rest of the night.

I didn't know it until the fighting was over, but Sergeant Wilson had been shot in the leg and had a deep cut on his left arm. During the battle, I heard bullets whizzing past me in all directions, but none of them found their mark. Praise the Lord.

At first light, the radio came to life.

"Forward Fire Base Delta Tango this is the USS Southland DD 743, over." "USS Southland this is Forward Fire Base Delta Tango. Boy are we glad to hear from you, over."

"Delta Tango we have been steaming all night. We heard you could use a little help up here, over."

"Southland you've got that right. We have some uninvited guests that want to crash our party. If you could lay in a little

VT frag (anti-personnel projectiles) or maybe some H.E. (High Explosives) at co-ordinance Alpha 3 Charlie 6 on map Zulu 25. Fire one round for effect, over."

A minute later the tree line two hundred yards to the north of the camp became just so many toothpicks.

"Right on the money Southland. Continue from that co-ordinance and work your way toward Alpha 3 Charlie 8, over."

"Alpha 3 Charlie 8, affirmative."

The exploding shells, besides clearing the forest, would often be followed by the sight and sound of secondary explosions, meaning that the shells were landing on enemy positions and setting off their munitions or fuel supplies. The bombardment continued for the better part of an hour then just as quickly as it had started it was over. An eerie silence fell over the whole area, not even the birds could be heard.

"Delta Tango, we'll stay on station for a few hours in case you need us, over." "Thanks, Southland. That was some fine shooting. We appreciate knowing you Navy boys got our backs. We're about down to throwing stones at the enemy, over."

"Our pleasure, Southland, over and out."

The shelling had barely subsided before helicopters started arriving with supplies.

They flew out the wounded and dead soldiers. As the Choppers flew in and out of the base, they swung over the area that the Navy had bombarded to see what they could see. The pilots of the helicopters reported seeing a lot of dead bodies and destroyed equipment, but they saw no live NVA Either they all died, or the ones that could, escaped back across the DMZ.

The Sarge received a purple heart for wounds he sustained which included a gunshot in the right leg and a stab wound to his left arm just below the shoulder. He was also awarded a silver star for his service on the night of the battle. More importantly, his reputation as an expert with a KA-Bar and a soldier with ice water in his veins went ahead of him wherever he went."

"That's the way I remember it," Jack concluded.

"Enough reminiscing, Jack let's get moving. We have an appointment with some troublemakers from the north.

WELCOME TO THE JUNGLE

The humidity was especially high because it had rained most of the night. A strong odor of wet and decaying leaves mixed with the aroma of tropical flowers hung heavy in the air. The lush green jungle canopy dotted with brilliantly colored flowers, dripped water incessantly on us as we made our way toward the objective. The mud stuck to our boots and made them feel like they weighed ten pounds each, and swarms of hungry mosquitoes were our ever-present companions.

As we proceeded deeper into the jungle the only sounds that could be heard were the dripping of the dew off the trees above, the sound of our boots on the soggy jungle floor, and the hum of the mosquitoes in our ears. I always found it fascinating that whenever there were men afoot in the jungle the birds and other animals would go silent. This behavior had proven beneficial to me in the past. On one occasion my squad had been hiding along a known artery of the Ho Chi Men Trail when an enemy patrol happened by. The enemy's presence was made known by the silence of the birds. We were able to capture the entire patrol without a single shot being fired. The information gained through the capture of the patrol saved many South Vietnamese and American lives.

There was an ever-brightening glow in the sky. Soon the sun would crest the hills to the east of the valley. This would make the enemy easier to spot, but it would also make us more vulnerable.

FRIEND OR FOE

06:15 6 June 1969 the sound of mechanized armor could be heard.
"What do you think Sarge, are they APC (armored personnel carriers), or Tanks?" "Can't tell for sure, Jack. That Chinese stuff the NVA uses all sound pretty much alike."

"One thing for sure Ken, if it's APC it could be bad, but if it's tanks it could be worse."

"What do you say, Jack, let's just get a positive ID on them. Call in an airstrike and get the hell out of Dodge."

....

"Roger that Sarge, I heard they're serving Sloppy Joes for lunch. If we could make it back for chow, I'd be a happy camper."

I'd never been the cause of a friendly fire incident, and I wasn't going to take the chance of causing one then. I figured we would make visual contact in about a hundred more yards. The military had gotten better at keeping track of where their troops were at any given time, but the system wasn't perfect, particularly when it came to the communication between the different branches of the military.

06:20 6 June 1969 it is full daylight and the stakes in this game of cat and mouse had gone to a whole new level. Every man in my squad was on high alert. They knew that in the light of day they could be spotted much easier so they were ever vigilant for any patrols the enemy might have to scout their route down the valley. Sweat beaded on each man's brow, not just from the heat, but from pure anxiety. The enemy was so close that I could smell their diesel exhaust in the air.

"Come on Sarge, call in an airstrike and let's get out of here."

"No Jack, I won't call for a strike until I have visual confirmation. It could be a South Vietnamese unit."

I wouldn't abandon the sacred oath I'd sworn to myself, that I'd never call fire on a position until I had a visual confirmation that it was the enemy.

DAYLIGHT DISASTER

Suddenly the unthinkable, Ka-boom! A huge explosion and the radioman had vanished. At first, we thought we were under fire, but the soldier closest to the man that had been vaporized told us that he heard a definite click before the blast. I knew that the French had mined this part of the country back when they were fighting the V. C. and from the amount of damage this mine did, it must have been an anti-tank mine. We didn't have time to stand around and ponder what had just happened. The chances were that there was a very large NVA force less than a click away and there was no doubt that they heard the explosion.

I gathered the men around and said, "I remember a rock outcropping about three-quarters of a mile back in the direction from which we came. I want everyone to head in that direction."

Jack is a full-blooded Cherokee Indian, and his tracking skills had saved our hides on more than one occasion. So, this was a no-brainer.

"Jack, take point and I will bring up the rear to make sure none of the new guys get lost."

"Ok, Sarge. You heard the man. Follow me and try and keep up."

Three-quarters of a mile through the jungle is not exactly a walk in the park, but when your fight or flight instinct kicks in and your adrenalin go through the roof it's amazing how much ground you can cover in a very short time. The vines tried to trip us, and the branches would grab at us, scratching our faces and hands, but we would not be denied. Every man was going to get to that rock out-cropping come hell or high water.

Ka-boom! Another explosion but this one was behind us. It was followed by multiple screams of men obviously in excruciating pain. The cries and yelling voices were Vietnamese. Jack and I were both pretty sure what that meant. The force we had heard was V.C. or more likely NVA. The enemy had stumbled across the same minefield that we had hit earlier. This was good news. Probably the only good news my men and I were likely to get all day. The explosion would slow the enemy down. They would have to deal with their wounded and they would have to sweep for more mines if they planned on bringing their mechanized armor to bear on us.

Jack and the rest of the men reached a small clearing in the jungle; probably a old rice paddy. On the other side was the rock outcropping that they were looking for. "Alright men, Jack said, take up positions among the rocks and spread out so the V.C. thinks there are more of us than there are."

In the meantime, I was getting a little surprise for the NVA. I had brought three claymore mines along just in case. Normally I wouldn't bring anything like this because of the weight but knowing the size of the force we were looking for I decided that if things went wrong the claymores might help even up the odds. I strategically placed the claymores for maximum damage on the enemy force. Once done, I made my way across the field to where the rest of the men were positioned.

SAFE OR SORRY

No radio, no way of signaling for help, outnumbered ten to one, and we weren't even supposed to check in for another hour. I knew this would probably turn out to be one of the worst spots that Jack and I had ever been in. I wasn't sure if we should have made our stand in the rock out-cropping or if we should have just kept running. It was the high ground and the rocks provided good cover, still, I couldn't help but wonder if, at the end of the day, we would be safe, or sorry. I figured that with a little luck and the use of the claymores we might just survive long enough for help to arrive.

I was counting on the fact that if we didn't contact our base on time they would send out a search party. The only flaw in the plan was the fact that we may not be alive by the time they sent someone looking for us. But that was a chance we took every day. It's called war.

The sun was climbing higher in the sky. The sky was blue and cloudless, and on any other occasion this would have qualified as a beautiful day, but all I could hear, running through my mind was, "this is a good day to die".

"Corporal, pass the word for the men to check their weapons, count their ammo, and make every shot count."

"Will do Sarge; those Claymores were a nice touch." "Thanks, Jack, Let's just hope they'll make the difference."

I remembered thinking that if l ran out of bullets, I would still have my trusty KA-Bar knife. When things got rough, I had always relied on my training, luck, and my KA-Bar. Jack on the other hand trusted in the Lord. He always prayed before a mission and especially just before and sometimes during a big fight.

I had mocked him on more than one occasion and said, "When your number is up, it's up."

But Jack would just smile and say, "God loves you, Ken."

I used to find that most irritating, but I knew Jack had a good heart and he meant well, so I would just pretend that I didn't hear it and I'd go about my business.

"Here they come!" someone said in a voice loud enough for us to hear but not so loud as to give away our position.

Just then the tree line on the other side of the clearing erupted in gunfire. The NVA was well equipped with AK-47s and a couple of heavy machine guns. This was when I was glad that my men were all Green Berets. As I looked down the line I didn't see a single look of panic or even fear, just a look of determination on the faces of every man in the unit.

"Fire at will," I shouted.

With that, the men started firing. They had all set their M-16s on the single-shot instead of full auto, which was where they would normally have them set. They picked their targets and made every shot count, just as I had ordered. The enemy forces were gathering along the tree line in preparation for a massive frontal attack. The enemy unit was moving men up from the rear faster than my men could fell them.

When I thought the enemy had enough men at the edge of the clearing to start their charge, I set off my little surprise.

"Fire in the hole!"

Click, Click, Click, Ka-boom! The sound of three claymores going off at the same time was deafening. The rock out-cropping was shaped like an amphitheater and the sound reverberated off of every rock. The enemy didn't know what hit them. All they knew was their force had been decimated, so they sounded the retreat. I knew this was a short-lived victory, but I was glad for a lull in the action.

When the smoke cleared all that remained on the other side of the clearing were dead body's two badly mangled heavy machine guns and some burning bushes. After a quick headcount, I was relieved to know that all my men were alive and well. Though I didn't show it, I cared about them a great deal. Jack and I had long since stopped trying to learn every man's name, and we avoided learning any more personal history than we had to. I had started the day with four privates and two corporals not including Jack and myself. The radioman was a corporal from Texas, so Jack and I referred to him as Tex. Everyone got a nickname usually denoting where he came from. There was Tex, who worked on a ranch near Austin. Kansas, whose family owned a thousand-acre corn farm, Phil, short for Philadelphia, who had worked in a deli, before he got his letter from Uncle Sam, Florida, who dropped out of college to join up, Homer, and Big Foot. The next to the last guy got his name because of what he could do. He was the camp home run champion, and the last guy wore a size fifteen boot.

Jack made his way down the line and said, "Keep a sharp lookout, and keep your KA-Bar at the ready."

Jack and I knew the next time the enemy came at us they wouldn't stop till they finished the job. By my estimation, between the claymores and my men, we had dispatched at least a hundred of the enemy. There were still enough NVA to mount another attack and they had not used their mechanized armor or even their mortars yet. This thought troubled me deeply, but I didn't let my concerns be known by the men.

I had toyed with the idea of sending one of my men as a runner back to base to get help, but with an opposing force as large as the one we were facing I knew we needed every man and every gun. The position I had chosen to fight from was a good one from a defensive perspective, but it left very little in the way of escape routes if the battle went badly. All Jack and I could hope for were that enough time would elapse before we were over-run, that the C.O. would call for a surveillance plan to try and locate our position.

An hour and a half had already passed since we had taken up our position so I was hoping someone would be looking for us soon; preferably before the enemy returned.

HELL IN THE AFTERNOON

It was twelve-thirty and except for a few pot-shots fired in our direction to make us keep our heads down and forget about trying to make a break for it, the NVA had been very quiet.

I knew because of the shape of the rock formation we were in that the enemy would have a hard time flanking our position. Unless they planned on pulverizing me and my men with tank fire, the enemy would have no choice but to attack from the front again. This had proved to be very costly to them in the morning. I didn't dare to hope that the NVA would just pass us by and continue on their way. I knew the enemy couldn't afford to let us escape and get word back to the base about the size of the NVA force or the direction they were heading.

I knew the next charge would be the last, so I said, "Men put your guns back on full auto, fix your bayonets, and get ready to use your hand-grenades."

The words had no sooner left my mouth until ... "Incoming!"

The word that every soldier dreads; this word foretells of a large artillery shell, bomb, or in this case, a mortar round bound toward our position. Ka-boom! The shell landed just short of our position and slightly to the left. Each man had his spot and all of them should survive anything but a direct hit. As I looked around at my men, they all appeared to be hunkered down and ready for the mortar assault. When I turned back, I saw Jack praying. I didn't know whether to be angry or jealous. I had always felt that the God thing was just a bunch of you know what, and that only a weak person needed it to lean on. For some unknown reason on that day, I felt differently. I wondered what Jack had, that I didn't. I remembered how Jack would finish his prayer just before a battle, and a look of total peace would come over him. I wished I had that peace right about then, because it was about to get ugly, and I knew it. Ka-boom! Another mortar round, this one hit just long, but the dead center of the rock outcropping we were using as shelter.

I yelled, "Keep your heads down men. When this is over, they'll make their charge."

Ka-boom! This one was right on the money. Fortunately, it missed everyone's position and did no harm, but the enemy had the range and the wind gauge, so now it was just a matter of time. Luckily mortars aren't as accurate as rifles or even cannons, so if one kept his head down, and luck was on his side, he could survive a mortar barrage. The mortars fell like rain causing the rocks that the Green Berets had taken refuge among to break off in chunks and fly in every direction. The men were getting pummeled by the stone fragments, and if they didn't have on helmets and flak jackets more than one man could have been badly hurt. As it was, no one received more than a couple of bruises and some scratches. I had taken up a position right next to Jack, and during the bombardment, one mortar shell had zeroed in on us. I saw this one coming and I knew Jack and I had no chance. Then it happened.

AMAZING GRACE

If anyone had told me this story, I wouldn't have believed a word of it, but it happened to me, and I saw what I saw with my own eyes. At an altitude of about twenty feet, the mortar exploded. This doesn't normally happen. The mortar shells the enemy used that day were contact weapons and generally explode when they hit the ground.

The fact that it exploded prematurely, unusual though that may be, is not the amazing part of the story. The amazing part is that when it exploded, caught in the flash was the silhouette of a man wearing a long flowing robe with his arms outstretched. The mortar seemed to explode against his body and the shrapnel bounced back in the other direction.

Jack saw what I saw, but all the other men had their heads down. When our eyes met, I knew that Jack knew what I had seen, and he just smiled. Jack's eyes glowed with the glow of someone who knew Jesus and had seen one of God's miracles up close and personal.

A few more shells fell before the sound of a Huey gunship could be heard. It opened up on the enemy mortar position with its machine guns and rockets. No more mortars fell on the rock out-cropping. Suddenly the sound of a pair of F-4 Phantoms could be heard screaming down the valley just above the trees. The jungle on the other side of the clearing exploded in flames as the jets dropped napalm on the NVA position. Two more Huey's swooped in and landed in the clearing while the gunship circled above.

No one needed a special invitation to run for the choppers and catch a ride home.

Within two minutes all the men were on board and the birds were in the air. As they exited the area l could see the phantoms returning time and again to wreak havoc on the enemy.

By the time a ground force was sent to the area to mop up, the battle-hardened NVA had lost their will to fight. Only thirty men were left alive out of a force of nearly five hundred and they had had enough. When the American forces arrived, the enemy soldiers were sitting in the middle of a field with their weapons piled up in a large heap some twenty feet away.

As the Choppers flew above the lush green canopy of the Vietnamese jungle, the wind swirled all about the cabin. The doors were open to accommodate the machine guns mounted on either side. I didn't see the guns. I didn't even hear the engines or feel the wind. All I could see was the beauty all around. The green of the forest below, the bright blue sky above, and the smiling faces of my men, all of whom had made it out safely. I knew it wasn't my brilliance as a military tactician or even dumb luck. I knew that Jack was right all along. There was a God in the heavens, and on that day, He had seen fit to save a sinner named Ken Wilson from certain death. Never had I seen a more beautiful day.

FROM HELL TO HALLELUIAH

I had always thought that when you die, that was it. I never allowed myself to think that there might be something beyond death. It was hard to earn my respect much less my friendship. I didn't let very many people close, because I had learned as a child how painful it was to lose a friend. Jack had indeed joined the ranks of a small club when he earned my friendship. Today I was the one that thought myself fortunate to have a friend in Jack Sullivan.

Jack had grown up on the reservation in the beautiful mountains of North Carolina. Jack's family didn't have much money and his dad was out of work more than he worked, but Jack never felt that he lacked for anything. His parents, and in particular, his mother were godly people. Jack's Mom made sure that he was in church every Sunday.

When Jack was ten years old, he had a Sunday school teacher that explained the Gospel of Jesus to his class. At the end of the class, she asked if anyone wanted to ask Jesus into their heart.

Jack was the only one in the class that said yes, so she dismissed the other children and led Jack through the prayer of salvation. Jack was on his knees repeating what the teacher was saying and meaning every word when he felt something like warm oil being poured over his head and flowing to his toes. Jack didn't know what it was, but he knew what it meant, and he has followed the Lord from that day on. Now it was Jack's turn to show me the way. Jack had led a hand full of people to the Lord, but never anyone that had been so set against it as I was.

When the C.O. Major Charles Jackson, didn't hear from us on schedule he knew that we were in trouble. I had been assigned to his camp for four months and had never failed to check in on schedule. Major Jackson ordered the Huey's to head toward the valley where my squad and I were going, to make sure everything was all right. The Major contacted the airbase at Da Nang and asked to have a couple of F-4 Phantoms fueled, armed, and sitting on the runway in case the Huey's called for backup. We heard about this during our debriefing, and I thought to myself. *It pays to be punctual.*

After the men were debriefed, we had some chow. During chow, the men in my unit all gathered around the table that Jack and I were eating at and started sounding off.

" You showed them, Sarge."

"I never thought we'd get out of that one Sarge, but you pulled us through." "I thought we were goners for sure, but here we are Hot Dam!"

"I' d march into Hell with you Sarge."

" You're one cool character, Sergeant Wilson. Yes indeed, one cool Character."

I smiled and nodded as the men filed by, but I knew it wasn't my brilliant military strategy that had saved us. It was nothing short of divine intervention. After the men had left the mess hall,

I asked Jack to take a walk. I had lots of questions and I hoped Jack would be able to answer them to my satisfaction. Neither of us mentioned the miracle that we had witnessed that afternoon, during the debriefing for fear of getting discharged on a section eight.

When I was sure we were well out of earshot of anyone in the camp I let fly with my questions.

"Jack, what happened this afternoon? Did I see what I think I saw? Was that ah, ah, Jesus?"

"Slow down Sarge, I can only answer one question at a time. Yes, you witnessed a miracle today. God has a plan for your life and the plan didn't include dying this afternoon."

"What plan is that? I never even knew He existed until today."

"The Lord works in mysterious ways his wonders to perform", Jack said. "What is that supposed to mean?"

"It means God is God and it isn't our place to question what He does or why."

"But why me, Jack? I've never done anything but give you and anyone else that believed in Him a hard time."

"You don't have to tell me," Jack said with a chuckle in his voice. "I was there. All I know is you and I are standing here right now for a reason. We should be dead, and there is no denying that."

"You're right Jack. I owe my life to Jesus and maybe I should give my life to Him as you have."

"Maybe you should Ken. Maybe you should."

THE REBIRTH OF KEN WILSON

From that day forward I couldn't get enough of Jesus, and the Bible. On 10 June 1969, I got down on my knees and ask the Lord into my heart. The next day Jack, the Chaplin from the Air Force Base at Da Nang, and I went down to China Beach on the South China Sea where Kenneth Wilson was baptized Kenneth (Paul) Wilson. After hearing the story of my miraculous conversion, the Chaplin thought that Paul would be the perfect Baptismal name to give me since my story so closely resembled St. Paul's conversion on the Damascus Road.

Following my rebirth, Jack and I would do Bible studies together and we would have a long conversation about what we had read. I was so sold on Jesus that I convinced Jack to help me start a Bible Study Class for the men in the unit and anyone else on the base who wanted to attend. As you can guess, this was met by more than a little skepticism. My reputation as a beer-guzzling, card playing, ladies' man, was well known and my persona as a stone-cold killer didn't help either. It took a lot of convincing to get the men to believe that it wasn't some kind of joke. Some of the comments went as follows:

"Next you'll be telling us you've given up booze and broads."

"Sergeant Wilson, alias "The Slasher", come to God, I don't believe it." "What you been smoking, Jack; Sergeant Wilson a Christian, Ha!"

"I've heard it all now. The Sarge, in church, that'll be a cold day in Hell."

Despite all the initial resistance, within a month and a half, some of the men in the camp were coming to Bible Study regularly, and when we weren't on patrol on Sundays Jack, and I would conduct a layman's church service. I still enjoyed a cold beer from time to time, but my days of gambling and Bargirls were over. I would spend most of my R&R time sitting under a tree or lying in a hammock reading the Bible.

Jack soon went from teacher to student, as I had been blessed with an uncanny understanding of the Bible and the messages that it was trying to convey to sinful man. My prayer life, which had been non-existent, became a mainstay in my life. I went from short formal prayers, when I was first saved, to long conversations with the Lord.

As I grew in the Word, Jack told me that he would often see me strolling by myself and carrying on what appeared to be a two-sided conversation with some unseen person. I would just smile and say that I was talking to Jesus.

Jack and I survived our time in Vietnam and through our efforts many lives were changed. My trusty KA-Bar got a lot of use after my rebirth. Not for killing people, although I must confess that I had to use it for that a few times after my conversion, but for whittling little wooden crosses out of some of the native hardwoods. Every time someone came to Jesus, I would make them a cross and carve their initials into it. I gave away hundreds of little crosses before my tour of duty was up. I'm fluent in Vietnamese and I'd make every effort to talk to the prisoners about Jesus. By my count, I led thirty-two VC to Christ before I left Vietnam.

    Jack and I were to get discharged immediately upon returning to the States and both of our tours were up on the same day. My parents were dead. Dad died in a car crash and Mom had developed pneumonia after catching the flu and died in 1967. I didn't want to go back to L.A., so Jack invited me to come home with him. This sounded good to me, so that was that.

AMERICA THE BEAUTIFUL

Back in the beautiful mountains of North Carolina, Jack and I took time to fish in the crystal clear and very cold streams around Jack's home. Jack had inherited a couple of acres just off the reservation from an uncle who had died after Jack graduated from school and just before he joined the Army. The property came complete with a modest two-bedroom log cabin situated right on top of a mountain.

"Jack, why did your uncle build his home on the top of a mountain?" "Well, Sarge, he did it to be closer to God."

"That makes perfect sense to me now, but had you told me that before I saw Jesus I would have laughed till I cried."

"I know Ken. A lot of things change when you allow Jesus to come into your heart."

"You're telling me. My hopes, dreams, and desires have changed since I found Jesus."

"You mean when you use to hope for a straight flush, dream of some barmaid, and desire a cold beer?"

"Ok. You got me on that one, but yes, that's exactly what I mean. Now I only want to know the Lord better and help others to know him as I do."

Jack and I would often hunt, with a camera. Neither of us could bring ourselves to shoot one of God's creatures after the death and suffering we had witnessed, and even inflicted during the war. The abundance of wildlife near Jack's home provided us with some amazing shots. Some of the pictures hang in my office at the church, even today.

My walk with the Lord became even closer, during long forages into the forest around Jack's home. The beautiful colors of the fall leaves and the majesty of the snow covered mountains in the winter made me wonder how I could have ever been so blind to the wonder of God's glorious creations. On more than one occasion while sitting by a tree, reading my bible, and chewing on some boiled peanuts which had become a favorite of mine since I was introduced to them by Jack; I would look up to see a squirrel or a couple of chipmunks looking for a handout. On one occasion an overly curious chipmunk crawled in the bag of peanuts and went rolling down the hill bag, peanuts, and all. I laughed so hard I had tears running down my cheeks. Those memories will be ones I treasure forever.

Jack and I both planned to use the G I Bill to further our educations. Jack was vacillating between becoming a teacher or a pilot. I, on the other hand, knew exactly what I wanted to be. I wanted to become a preacher so I could share the joy that I had discovered in Jesus Christ with anyone and everyone that would listen.

LASER FOCUS

After giving ourselves almost a year to unwind and try to put the war behind us, Jack and I decided to get on with our lives. I was laser-focused on what I wanted to do. I was going to go into the clergy. I enrolled in a Bible college in East Tennessee and began my studies. Jack still couldn't decide between teaching and becoming a pilot.

So, I said, "Why don't you learn how to fly and then teach flying?"

Jack couldn't believe how insightful that was. Jack did what I suggested, and you can find him at Blairsville Municipal Airport, N.C. six days a week. He loves to teach flying but not even flying will keep him out of Church on Sunday. I graduated at the top of my class thanks to the Lord, and shortly after graduation I was asked to preach in the Church I still shepherd today.

Jack, his wife, and their two girls visit me and my church quite often. Jack did me the honor of letting me perform his wedding ceremony and I was at the hospital for the birth of both of his daughters. His wife Sue is just as nice as she is beautiful. She is a full-blooded Cherokee just like Jack and theirs is a beautiful family, full of love and God's grace.

Jack and I seldom talk about the old days of the war, but I have a reminder of my old life in a glass case on my desk. In it are my trusty KA-Bar, my dog tags, and one of the little wooden crosses I carved in Vietnam. On a brass plate secured to the box is the inscription; *From a KA-Bar to the Cross.*

POSTSCRIPT

I hope you have enjoyed reading *From a KA-Bar to the Cross*. All the Characters are fictional as are all the events. The locations are real, but any similarity to anyone living or dead is strictly coincidental.

Although the miracle which was depicted in the book was nothing more than a figment of my imagination; I do believe that miracles do happen daily in this world. Although the age of signs and wonders is over, I believe that God is still in the miracle business. If this book causes one person to seek the Lord, then I consider that a miracle.

The story of Jack's salvation as a child is my story, but other than our love of the Lord there are no similarities between Jack and me. I'm Irish American.

www.ingramcontent.com/pod-product-compliance
Lightning Source LLC
LaVergne TN
LVHW020440080526
838202LV00055B/5283